Murder Must Appetize

Books by H. R. F. Keating

Murder
Must Appetize

by H. R. F. KEATING

H. R. F. Keating

New York
THE MYSTERIOUS PRESS

1981

London
LEMON TREE PRESS

First published in 1975 by The Lemon Tree Press, Ltd., London. Revised edition first published in 1981 simultaneously by The Lemon Tree Press, Ltd., London, and The Mysterious Press, New York.

FIRST EDITION IN THE UNITED STATES OF AMERICA
ISBN 0 89296 053 1 The Mysterious Press (Limited edition)
ISBN 0 89296 052 3 The Mysterious Press (Trade edition)
ISBN 0 904291 05 7 The Lemon Tree Press
Library of Congress Catalogue Card Number 81-83116

The Mysterious Press
129 West 56th Street
New York, N.Y. 10019

The Lemon Tree Press
Basset Chambers
27 Bedfordbury
London WC2N 4BJ

Murder Must Appetize

HULBERT FOOTNER

Author of
THE OWL
TAXI

EASY TO KILL

IS there anything, when life gets a little much, as
comforting as a detective story? Well yes, of course
there is. Drink. The love of a good woman. The
attentions of a bad woman. Yet for many of us the
quintessential detective story does have a warm in-
ward spreading cosiness that can expel any number of
everyday horrors. It is worth asking just how these
curious concoctions come to have such magical
powers.

But first, what is the quintessential 'tec? For me, it
should come more or less from the half-decade leading
up to World War II. Perhaps this is only because this
was when I first began to read—no, gobble—the
genre. The scent of those first fine careless rootlings,
rising again, fills my head with old, forgotten, far-off
things and murders long ago. It is that heads-you-win,
tails-you-win nostalgic feeling either for times that
were good and cannot by anything ever be taken
away from us or for times that were bad and have
been gone through and successfully come out of. Yet
perhaps there are good reasons for the delightfulness
of that generation of what are nowadays called crime
books.

Reflections on a golden age

Learned critics—and even crime fiction has its sprink-
ling of these—begin the golden age of the detective
story a good deal earlier than my chosen heyday. They
argue that the form came to its full characteristic
growth about 1920 with as a culminating point the
foundation in 1928 of the Detection Club, a solemnly
elected body of masters, a sort of dining Académie
Policière, which when it drew up rules in 1932, stated
firmly, 'it is a demerit in the detective novel if the
author does not "play fair".' But even in the most
24-carat time of the golden age, its rules were broken,
and by its most successful practitioners.

As early as 1926 Agatha Christie wrote *The Murder
of Roger Ackroyd*, the one where—I don't care if I am
giving it away—the Watson done it. And Dorothy
Sayers, co-queen of that golden reign, was equally
busy infringing her own edicts, first declaring that a
love interest was quite unacceptable and then in 1930
going so unutterably far as to let her detective, the all-
solving Lord Peter Wimsey, fall in love with the chief
suspect. But this was only the crowning moment of a
process she had long been allowing to creep onwards,
the head of the worm i' the bud.

What she was doing was to let people, recognizably
real people, play havoc with the purity of the puzzle.
And a splendid thing that was. When you can get
people into those conjurings-up of imaginary worlds
that are works of fiction, you get things that have a
life of their own. And these were what we loved.
Books that first declared their limitations by announc-
ing themselves as detective stories, thus promising the
exclusion of certain aspects of existence, but then sur-
prised us with lifelike life to mull over deliciously on
our long country walks. Well, that's what we did in
those distant days.

The emergence of the appetizing murder

Take Miss Sayers' *Murder Must Advertise*, in many ways the pattern of all we hoped for from the treasure trove we lugged away on our weekly visits to W. H. Smith's or Boots' Libraries (the public library was regarded as a little bit 'common', essence of the thirties word). It came out in February 1933 and was reprinted again in that June and again in a cheap edition in January 1934 and by July 1939 had reached its tenth impression (two shilling edition). Dorothy L.

DEATH IN THE CLOUDS

AGATHA CHRISTIE writes her greatest Poirot Story

" It is always a delight to meet Hercule Poirot again. . . . He is one of the few detectives with real charm."
—Dorothy L. Sayers

" Mrs. Christie is evidently as much in love with her Belgian detective as all her admirers are, and an additional warmth creeps into her writing when she writes of him."
—Edward Shanks

Back cover to an early Christie

Sayers was hailed by many as the finest detective-story writer of the century, treated by the newspapers as an absolute oracle and finally stepped into the successive shoes of G. K. Chesterton and Edmund Clerihew Bentley, author of *Trent's Last Case*, as President of the Detection Club.

I imagine that what most of us who remember *Murder Must Advertise* recall is its setting of the agency into which Lord Peter was planted as a temporary copywriter to investigate the mysterious death of his predecessor. But there is, in fact, a second substantial strand to the book, a highly romantic to-do over drug smuggling with Lord Peter, mostly dressed as a harlequin, dashing about a lot in a powerful car. It is odd how the whole drugs business appears in the light literature of the twenties and thirties, looked at from the standpoint of today. Then it was cocaine that was smuggled rather than heroin, though of course the two are equally destructive and addictive. Yet the detective-story writers let their major characters take to 'coke' and kick it with little apparent effect. Only vignette baddies were allowed to perish from it. The phenomenon begins as early as the great hypodermic fetishist, Sherlock himself. There was never a sign there of nausea and imaginary ants crawling beneath the skin when suddenly the game was afoot. And, equally, the lady who 'doped' in *Murder Must Advertise*, the notorious Dian de Momerie, never seemed more the worse for wear than would be accounted for by prolonged 'ginning it up', and she ended her short life decently murdered.

Miss Sayers drew an explicit parallel in the book between this unlikely tosh-bosh and her much more convincing advertising world, and she said in a piece she wrote in 1937 that the whole thing had been intended as 'a criticism of life'.

Reading it again today, one sees what she meant.

But, truth to tell, although the material is there in the shape of occasional swoops into solemn discussion sessions on advertising ethics and fine old rhetorical montages of questionable slogans, somehow the criticism does not really happen. You are not left, as you are with your top novelists and even with the best of the crime writers of today, with a sense of something said coming from every event, every facet of character, every phrase of description. But, on the other hand, you do get a highly entertaining story, indeed an appetizing one, that scurries you along by the pull of its puzzle while giving you telling sketches of true-life people and of the way they lived at least in their open hours.

All this and Lord Peter Wimsey too. His Lordship was no doubt a great attraction, though looking back analytically I am not sure that the highly characterised detective—your Wimsey, your Poirot, your Mr Campion—was the true nub of the delight. Certainly such a figure was more or less a necessity, and they existed in great variety from Wimsey, appealing simultaneously to the snob within and to the inner little man who finally turns the tables (alas, more often in imagination than in reality), to figures hardly rising above the general dullish level of their authors' other characters yet still designed to hold a following. But the hero-detective then was, I think, more in the nature of a brand label than something appreciated solely for himself. With a St Michael sign on the book you knew you would get Marks and Spencer quality through and through.

Life in the not so raw
What in retrospect looms larger than the detective in these thirties stories is the Background, that setting which, avid all the while to find out who had done it, we absorbed painlessly and joyously. But the back-

ground was not so much the details of advertising practice or bellringing nomenclature or riding the Orient Express or vicarage, hospital or Oxford life or the ins-and-outs of a Mayfair fashion-house, of which the facts at least are all quickly forgettable; no, it was the people in their settings.

The door opened noiselessly and Lord Peter Wimsey walked in. "How did you get here?" exclaimed Parker.

Yet it was not the whole of each person either. In *Murder Must Advertise* the character of the tormented Tallboy (you never get to know his Christian name: that's the way it was in them thar days) is well enough drawn and has been praised in print. He is lifelike all right, ready to go with a flighty bit while his wife is

having the baby, proud and ashamed of Dumbleton, his second-rate public school, but he is never a deathless creation. Oh, but Dumbleton! What a clue that made-up place-name provides to Miss Sayers' snobbery and to ours then. And how it takes one back to those good old class-conscious days. We are told that the class system still flourishes, and maybe it does. But we have really emerged from the era when a writer could let her characters seriously discuss, as Miss Sayers unblushingly does and as more than one other detective story practitioner did too, just to what extent one of them was 'not quite a gentleman' and what he could possibly do about the stigma.

But, re-reading Tallboy today, we recognize that if we ever supposed he was one of the unforgettable creatures of a writer's imagination, he just is not. Nor did we ever want him to be. What we wanted was a certain happy crudity in our pictures. We wanted them to be vivid, as vivid as could be got. And we wanted them to be lifelike, but not as lifelike as could be got. Life had, and has, some very uncomfortable chunks in it.

The tunnel of death revisited

Perhaps to make clearer what these books did for us we should look at one of the ones which, though published during our chosen period, really dated from the earlier era. Things are never as cut-and-dried as, in kindness to the meticulous literary historian, they ought to be. However, my curiosity aroused about just what it was I had loved, I disinterred from the shelves of the London Library a handful of run-of-the-mill thirties whodunits acquired in the days when that excellent institution had more about it of the gentleman's club than the scholar's reference machine. Among them was *Death in the Tunnel* by Miles Burton.

A railway timetable mystery this, a pure puzzle like

many that continued to be written well into the age of the book with a background, in much the same way as today you can find all new and fresh published genuine examples of the background-only crime story as it came once from the pen of Miss Dorothy L. (she was always, those who knew her tell me, very hot on the 'L') Sayers. And nice these often are too. Mr Burton's plot concerns a devilishly ingenious murder committed (and once more I don't care if I am giving it away) by halting a train in which the victim has just been shot by means of a red light dangled down the ventilation shaft of a tunnel on the end of 'an electric flexible' and then hauling up the murderer. There's cunning for you. But not enough to fool the patient, prolix and not very characterful Desmond Merrion, 'something of an amateur criminologist'.

The interest was in people
and their settings

And the book, like its detective, is, truth to tell, fairly high on dullness. How about this for a snappy start? 'The 5.0 p.m. train from Cannon Street runs fast as far as Stourford, where it is due at 6.7. On Thursday, November 14th, it was, as usual, fairly full, but not uncomfortably so.' Just look at all those helpful commas to guide us through the thickety prose.

For many a page the murder is dutifully supposed to be suicide. Although the victim is a bachelor of sixty, it is only in one hurried aside of 'no entanglements with women or anything like that' that the possibility is hinted at of his having killed himself because of an unconventional sex life, a suggestion which almost every crime writer of today would feel bound to pursue, often at length. When eventually Mr Burton does establish that there is a murder to investigate we set off on a round of suspects and witnesses, meeting the doctor who 'proved to be an elderly man of benevolent aspect' and some forty pages later a farmer, an elderly man of—guess what— 'benevolent aspect'. And at long last the mystery is solved (not without an acid marginal comment from some London Library reader of 'Improbable!') and the villains are arrested. 'They were duly hanged,' come the final words. Or, to quote from the last page of a similar opus, *Death at Breakfast* by John Rhode, 'He was tried for the murder of Victor Harleston, sentenced and executed.' We liked all the ends tied up, you see. But, to make assurance doubly sure, both books add those two words scarcely ever absent indeed from any of the products of that age, 'The End'.

'The atmosphere in the little room was electric'

Well, I suspect that if I ever did read *Death in the Tunnel* I was a little disappointed. We recognised that there could be comparative duds in our Boots'

Library treasure hauls. Yet even such a misfire had in it some of the ingredients we considered essential to our proper pleasure in the sort of book we really wanted. There was, first, the central detective, the figure, however improbable, who worked to convince us down there in the depths of our minds that we poor puny mortals could single-handedly smite Evil and chop it down. Usually, as here, the detective was an amateur, thus enabling us to identify with him more

easily and share his hunt through the pages. But, police or amateur, he had to possess two important qualities.

He had to be omniscient (Michael Innes said casually once of his detective, John Appleby, that he 'happened to know some Russian,' and that in 1937). And he had to be omnipotent; to quote again from Michael Innes, Mrs Platt-Hunter-Platt speaking, 'Exactly—a real detective. There is a very good man whose name I forget; a foreigner and very conceited —but, they say, thoroughly reliable.' Mr Innes was joking, but good jokes spring from exact reality and we really did like our Poirots to be, no higher praise, 'thoroughly reliable'.

"How is it you smell of cigarettes?"
he asked without looking at her.

Death in the Tunnel had, too, a good selection of suspects, and the unlikely situation of each having good reason to have killed the victim. We liked when we could get it our detective to arrange his case indeed so that it ended with a Grand Confrontation of all these suspects. Technically this was necessary since all the people likely to have done the murder had to be kept in play as long as possible. If in any detective story worth its salt a suspect was eliminated early on this simply meant that they were to be flung into the boiling again at a later stage to give off clouds of yet blacker suspiciousness at the final denouement when, to quote the typical Cyril Hare of *Death Is No Sportsman* (a trout fishing one), 'The atmosphere in the little room was electric.' And, of course, at this grand confrontation one should be delightfully yet infuriatingly aware that one's omniscient detective has known for at least fifty pages who really has done it.

Listen to Nicholas Blake's hero, Nigel Strangeways: 'Yes,' said Nigel gravely. 'I think I know who the murderer is. But I doubt if I can ever prove it. A question of proof—that's a good title for a detective story, if you ever write one—and I've got enough proof to fill an acorn.'

I think I know what the title of that book is—*A Question of Proof*. And I think I know, from the evidence of that nuggetty little phrase 'not enough to fill an acorn', who Nicholas Blake was: none other than Cecil Day-Lewis, eventually to become Poet Laureate. Yet perhaps a quote from another poet, Ogden Nash, is not exactly amiss here:

> . . . held their knowledge aloof
> Why, they say, why, Inspector, I knew all along it was
> he, but
> I couldn't tell you, you would have laughed at me
> unless I had absolute proof.

Crime and the Poet Laureate

But *A Question of Proof* is still one of the ones that, for all that it was written in 1935, can be read with considerable enjoyment today. Though only the first novel of its then impecunious author (he told me once that the idea of writing it came into his head daydreaming over the phrase 'I'd do anything for money'), it fulfilled almost every requisite of our curious canon. Nigel Strangeways, a sort of non-playing newspaper man (thus excluded from his creator's sharpish jibes at tasteless reporters) came with plenty of god-like wisdom and miscellaneous literary knowledge and with several omnipotently dealt-with mysteries already under his belt. And he had the near-obligatory eccentricity, a facet designed to humanise without minimising. This was a huge addiction to tea, though it turned out to be a trait that hardly paid its way and was later quietly dropped.

Then the book had a background that was just right, the life of a prep school such as the penniless poet had served his time in. Remarkably well described this is, too, with real feeling for boys en masse, nicely caricaturised portraits of a collection of typical masters of the period ('There are so few jobs going nowadays especially for older men') and with a splendid climactic description of a cricket match, even if it is only between boys and fathers, which brings out character as surely as sunshine brings out the smell of mown grass.

Added to all this there is a sweeping, and still perfectly effective, whodunit tug. Who done it? Well, perhaps not precisely. It is rather the more intriguing question of 'How on earth was it done?' How was the first murder committed in the hay-castle when apparently only the nice hero and the nice heroine, who is unfortunately married to the fearful old prig of a headmaster (so we know who the second victim will be), were the only ones who could have been there at what seems to be the only possible time? I think I won't give the answer away. That tickling question should remain the tease it is until the pages are irresistibly turned.

Today there is as well an interest the author can hardly have foreseen. His accurate rendering of contemporary manners gives us a whole minefield of delicious thirties atrocities. We get all the agonies of 'not quite a gentleman' already encountered in Dorothy Sayers (a not wholly likeable suspect betrays under police pressure 'a slight coarsening of accent' and even the local, destined-to-be-foiled Inspector pounces on that like a kite). Then we have some splendid, now almost forgotten words. There is 'bim'—how long ago it is since I heard that marvellously middle-class thinning down and respectabilising up of 'bum'. There is 'oick'—and alas the Leftish poet lets this pejorative description of someone not birth-endowed with middle-class mores go by without a murmur. And there is 'bolshie'—how that summons up all affronted stolidity standing aghast at even hinted doubt over the axioms of gentlemanliness and property-owning.

But, of course, the young poet and anonymous mystery author was a bit of a bolshie himself. Julian Symons, historian of the whodunit, has written of the shock he felt, remembered years after, when he found on Page 1 of this book the name of T. S. Eliot (in fact, his memory betrayed him: it is on Page 2 that a quotation from 'Prufrock' squeals out in the thirties torpor). Possibly even more complexion-purpling was a later likening of an incident to 'a surréaliste film'. But perhaps ruffled proprieties were restored with two words of Greek printed in their proper alphabet.

One last desirable attribute this Nicholas Blake debut also had. Its plot was diabolically involved. A whole final chapter was needed after the murderer had

CLIVE·UPTTON——26

been unmasked to unravel it all. I do not think we then positively demanded this sort of complexity, but our authors had to have recourse to it if they were to produce puzzles that would not only defeat us, as in the golden twenties had been the sole object (Ronald Knox once laid it down that the literature should be played like a game of cricket), but would also evoke as the last pages were hurried through the true, admiring 'Gosh, how fiendishly clever.'

The plot thickens
Take, as another example, the explanation of *Greek Tragedy* by G.D.H. and Margaret Cole, in that day awesome theoreticians of the Labour movement as well as prolific writers of whodunits that were at least full of recognizeable, if not particularly memorable, people. Provenly unmemorable, I hazard, because *Greek Tragedy* has in it a cruise-passenger with the odd name of Perronet, and from the subconscious of that obvious detective-story addict Iris Murdoch a quarter of a century later in *An Unofficial Rose* what should pop up as a character name but Peronett. The nub of the Coles' plot—and I boil it down more than a little —is that one Aveling, an obnoxious lecturer on the cruise, tells a sixth-former called Arkell that, for no very good reason, he is going overland from Athens to Delphi. Arkell tells Bradfield, a bolshie master from his school who happens to be camping nearby, and Bradfield decides, quite why is not too clear, to kidnap Aveling. He leaves him drugged and unconscious in some bushes, where of course he is found and murdered by a Greek sailor from the cruise ship with whose wife he has, as it so happens, been having an affair. No wonder only the astute (and pretty colourless) Inspector Wilson can get to the bottom of it all.

And no wonder that after the solution is announced a lot of heavy explanation takes place. I suppose we

Dennis Arundell brings Lord Peter Wimsey to life
in a 1937 production of 'Busman's Honeymoon'

liked this part, and even checked back to see whether the clues had been fairly put. Well, I cannot remember ever doing that myself. Except for one glorious occasion when I actually spotted the really vital one, the fact that in Dorothy Sayers' *Five Red Herrings* the colours in an abandoned landscape painting did not correspond with the tubes of oils left with it. The jubilation I experienced was later, when I came to write mystery stories in my turn, to present me with the agonising question of whether what was really wanted was a plot so cunningly judged that the reader, far from losing the cricket match, was subtly presented in the crucial over with a no-ball to swipe satisfyingly to the boundary.

The leisure activity of criminal detection

But, though I was no clue checker, there were certainly plenty of people who were, among them the reader of most of my London Library specimens who splattered the margin at the least suspicion of dicey play and who, lynx-eyed, seemed to miss nothing. The fact was that in those days we had time for such things. There was no television to claim our idle hours, and we were even allowed by public opinion to be idle. Look at all the detectives in these books who had— ah, happy memories—'a small private fortune'. It was no shame then to have no occupation, to be like so many of the characters in our reading 'of independent means', spending one's life doing no more than being a gentleman, or, for the more raffish like the deplorable Milligan in *Murder Must Advertise*, in being simply 'a well-known clubman', onerous task.

Yet perhaps, after all, really fairly onerous. Lord Peter Wimsey, himself a bit of a clubman, took, we know, infinite pains over every detail of dress, even if assisted by the faithful Bunter, so much so that he is able instantly to recognise from which hatter an almost obliterated topper comes and thus lead the police to the Mr Big of the dope smugglers. Indeed, Leisure bred, in such pursuits as it did allow, an extraordinary thoroughness. And absolute Leisure bred absolute thoroughness—at least if we are to believe Michael Innes in *Hamlet, Revenge* when he asserts about the traditions of the owners of Scamnum

"Go back to that flat you've just left," he shouted. "As fast as you can."

Court that they would prevent the airy Noel from touching a cricket bat or a tennis racket without making a resolute onslaught on county form . . . would send Elizabeth forward from Somerville next year miraculously perfected in sundry dreary Old and Middle English texts.

And a less awe-inspiring thoroughness worked equally, I think, among the less-exalted leisured classes. It worked, too, among those who provided, often as a hobby like the Coles, Ronald Knox, Michael Innes himself, Cyril Hare the working barrister, and many another, the preferred reading matter of these classes. The plotters worked like stink at their plots, poring over rail timetables (Bradshaw still was) and forensic medicine textbooks, devising whole cross-word-puzzles as mere side-issues, agonising over alibis and sweating blood, in a gentlemanly or ladylike way, over getting into or out of comprehensively locked rooms

However, though thoroughness often extended these essentially light-hearted productions to a length that today seems excessive, it was not always enough to get them to the distant target of Page 280 or 300. So the unfortunate authors would give us solemn half-pages of detailed description each time a new character appeared. Or they would embark every now and again on a thousand words or more of purely in-filling dialogue. These, seen from today, often reveal the most give-away social niceties. And, of course, we readers then did not dare skip: a clue might be con-cealed in the chatter. That beginner, Nicholas Blake, complains once of the sheer-length burden by having one of his schoolmasters—they all naturally read de-tective stories—draw attention to the way in which, so as to fill half a line, heroes invariably 'carefully selected a cigarette' although there could be little advantage in taking one Abdulla—remember Abdul-las?—rather than the exactly identical Abdulla next to it.

The upstairs and downstairs of old fashioned murder

To give us the leisure in which to unravel the lengthy and careful ravellings we had servants. Or at the least we had—oh, forgotten, marvellous and often doubt-less pretty slapdash lady—a cook-general. No chores, sapping away the day's minutes, for us. No, after dinner or lunch (but not, unless we were depraved, in the morning) we could settle down to a good 'tec,

to sheer enjoyment. And naturally in its pages we would find, faithful reflection of contemporary circumstances, servants too.

And, golly, how as readers we looked down on servants. There was, to begin with, an unwritten rule that they should never be the murderer. No, worse than this, it was once at least a written rule, written in America, that great democracy. There, S. S. Van Dine, creator of Philo Vance, super-snob and super-intellectual detective, in an essay under his own name of Willard Huntington Wright (and it's a nice bonus that two of the rule-givers should be, first, Mr Wright

"Ladies and gentlemens," Giuseppi called out, "ze police——"
"Quite so," came a deep, genial voice from the stairs; "the police."

and, second, Mr Wrong—E. M. Wrong, anthologist in 1926 of the Oxford University Press 'World's Classics' *Crime and Detection* volume) laid it down that having a servant do it was too easy since the murderer would not be 'a worth-while person'.

In real life, as reflected in these pages, we thought nothing too of pushing servants together into one bedroom, even on occasion fielding a substitute in a temporarily unoccupied bed as in Gladys Mitchell's *Laurels Are Poison*. Such bedrooms they were too, as Nicholas Blake put it of one of them 'resembling in its extreme narrowness and draughtiness nothing so much as a corridor in an express train'. And then when the poor domestics were not of any use, as out of term-time in Gladys Mitchell's book set in a teachers' training college, why, we simply put them on board wages till we wanted them again.

But I was discussing the necessary ingredients, though the next item, the police, relates clearly enough to the servants with their invariably comic speech and brainless behaviour ('The sergeant stared uncomprehendingly'—N. Blake). Indeed, the vicar's wife in *Death Is No Sportsman* unblinkingly asks that a constable be told off to fetch her a chair. Often the lower police ranks were the object of a condescension which cannot but raise a pained eyebrow in the last quarter of the twentieth century, like the mention of 'A Police-Constable who has read *Macbeth*' in one list of dramatis personae—these were a frequent feature, somehow comforting if only for recalling characters otherwise unmemorable who just might be the murderer.

An inspector palls
Police work as such did not much interest the crime writers of that day. Few cases were solved by anything approaching actual police methods and that thorough-

ness in mugging up a background seemed never to extend to this activity. Even when a police detective was the triumphing hero his methods were usually hailed as unorthodox. Cyril Hare has a local inspector, 'essentially a simple-minded man who had risen to his position by hard work', baffled altogether by 'a quality of elusiveness and subtlety' in Inspector Mallett of the Yard. And E. C. R. Lorac (only recently revealed to me as hiding the identity of a woman, Edith Caroline Rivett) makes her Inspector Macdonald a great solver of tricky literary crosswords, even if the solving entails recourse to his customary four-letter word 'Losh' as he enjoys his greatest pleasure, sitting in front of a wood fire with a book. Oh, Telly, where art thou? Oh, Permsoc, how far away thou art yet?

Indeed, almost the only truly likely piece of police procedure used was the business of 'calling in the Yard', the process which had just taken place when the elusive Inspector Mallett baffled his country cousin. A great crux this always was. A moment of suspense for us readers. Were we to discover that a local man had special attributes which might even make him into a new running hero, like Henry Wade's Inspector Poole or Christianna Brand's Inspector Cockrill? Or would the Chief Constable happen to have a friend who would turn out to be our old friend too—Wimsey, Miss Marple, Mr Campion, Doctors Fortune, Fell or Thorndyke, Ronald Knox's Miles Bredon or one Toby Dyke? Or would the Yard regretfully be summoned and Inspector Mallett (Mary Fitt had one of this name too), or Mitchell (either Josephine Bell's or E. R. Punshon's), or French, or Waghorn, or Grant (Josephine Tey's addition to the crowded ranks of Yard Scotsmen) or Detective Constable Bobby Owen (we were never too sure what rank did what) arrive to take over?

But eventually one way or another the Chief Con-

"*I* *suppose,*" *snapped* *the* *inspector,*
"*you're* *going* *to* *say* *you've* *never*
seen her *before.*"

stable, Major This or Colonel That, would make up his mind. Unless, as quite often happened, he investigated the affair himself, bringing to it all the explosive military qualities that the fiction writers of that day knew to be the necessary qualifications for this post. They were indeed fairly grossly caricatured

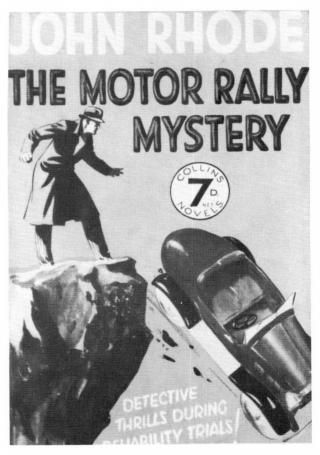

A suitable case for the Yard?

figures, these popping and barking military men, though the caricature can be amusing enough even forty years on. We did not, as I have said, demand great subtlety. The sort of characterisation we enjoyed was what Michael Innes, through the person of his detective-story writer Gott, once likened to a big splashy label like 'Bath Mat' on that necessary household item as opposed to the unembellished cork of the novel proper.

The late, lamented chapter heading

On a par with liking 'Bath Mat' characterisation we liked each chapter in our mysteries to have a title, where possible amusing, and followed by a dazzlingly apt quotation from the classics. Thus Anthony Gilbert, one of the notable women detective writers who continued the energy-filled adventures of her cheerfully vulgar solicitor Arthur Crook until her death in the early 1970s, produced at the heads of chapters in *Murder by Experts:* 'A woman doth the mischief brew, In nineteen cases out of twenty'—W. S. Gilbert; 'Something will come of this; I hope it mayn't be human gore'—Simon Tappertit (no reader forty years ago needed to be told he was a character in *Barnaby Rudge*); 'There is a passion for hunting something deeply implanted in the human breast'—*OliverTwist;* 'Altogether it's very bad weather, And an unpleasant sort of a night'—*Ingoldsby Legends.*

For examples of the sort of chapter titles that by oddness and aptness assured us we were on to the right thing I quote from Gladys Mitchell, another of the writers-then who are writers-now, creator of Mrs (later Dame) Beatrice Lestrange Bradley, cacklingly reptilian 'psychiatric adviser to the Home Office', a splendidly larger-than-life detective. From *Laurels Are Poison* we got: 'Intrusion of Serpents,' 'High Jinks With A Tin-opener', 'Revenge Upon Goldi-

In almost all circumstances
we took good care to wrap up well

locks', 'Skirling and Groans, 'Evidence of the Submerged Tenth', 'Iddy Umpty Iddy Umpty Iddy', and Chapter 15 'Rag', Chapter 16 'Bone'. Then there was as well 'Multiplicity of Promiscuous Vessels' as heading to a chapter in which chamber-pots played a major part but in which there was not a hint—dear, dead days gone by—of sexual promiscuity. Chamber-pots! What a source of innocent merriment they were in that once upon a time. Yet how many of them are there about today? Central heating, cosseting winter journeys from bed to loo, no doubt exiled thousands and mere change of fashion banished as many more, especially when servants to empty them also disappeared. But the world is a less mildly facetious place without them, and it is one of the nice small pleasures to recall their hilarious charm among the detective stories of yesterday.

Winter of content

And what about that chill outside the bedclothes? I suppose it still exists for some but by and large those squiggly little copper pipes have vanquished it. It is to be met, however, in its full hateful-pleasurable freezingness in these books. Casual references abound to fires—being poked, having to be lit, being let go out. Hot-water bottles too are filled and hugged between cold sheets. But even their comfort is not enough to repel the cold. When a mystery joker strikes in the college where *Laurels Are Poison* is set, what garments does he (or, as it turns out, she) cut and tear 'until they were quite beyond repair'? Why, nothing else than two pairs of heavyweight winter pyjamas.

In almost all circumstances in those days we took good care to wrap up well. Even at that college's dance the girls wore, as a lecturer who expected 'the silly fatheads' to catch rheumatism sitting out on the stairs gleefully said, 'nothing under their frocks except a pair of panties and a bust bodice'. And seldom indeed were any of us parted from our hats—man ('It requires the utmost strength of will to remain seated, and hatless'—*The Case of the Gilded Fly*), woman, even as young as twenty-six, ('In addition to these other discomforts she was wearing a tiresome hat'—*Laurels Are Poison*) or child ('Michael Evans, Esq., B.A., has just supervised the boys' changing . . . adjured A. not to go out without his hat . . .'—*A Question of Proof*). And when in *Murder by Experts* it was Chapter IV, 'Altogether it's very bad weather . . .', everybody

Reggie did not answer."

enveloped themselves in ulsters. From one of which a green button was in due course torn off . . .

Cold corpses, roast duck and green peas

But if a layer upon layer of clothing failed to ward off that chill there was always food, the so different, stodgy and plentiful middle-class food of the thirties. Inspector Mallett in *Death Is No Sportsman*, actually investigating a victim apparently dead of sunstroke, polished off first trout, poached from the high-priced stream on the banks of which the murder took place, and then 'a steaming steak and kidney pudding'.

Mrs Lestrange Bradley delighted the young narrator of *Laurels Are Poison* with tea consisting of 'toast, ham, boiled eggs, sardines, new bread, butter, honey and jam'. But I suppose she was lucky to get the new bread since the college bakehouse was used only twice a week, a crux of the mystery this and a fact that produced from the Lynx of the London Library two highly scornful marginal exclamation marks. However, each twice-weekly baking must have been on a massive scale. Bread was eaten at breakfast and tea of course and doubtless too at lunch and dinner. But then came supper, bread-and-butter, cocoa and biscuits.

These huge intakes are exceeded only by the luxurious meals which E. R. Punshon's young Detective Constable Bobby Owen, of the Yard, works his way through while providing protection for a retired City man. On the night his charge is murdered—here too it is high summer—the pair of them ate 'sole cooked in Madeira, roast duck served with green peas done in butter, apple tart with cream, followed by coffee obedient to the maxim of the Eastern sage that coffee should be 'as sweet as love, as black as night, as strong as death, and as hot as hell" '. How often, as a boy, did I hear that maxim fall from my father's lips. It takes me back, it takes me back.

"*I shall be seriously disappointed,*" she said, "*if it does not turn out to be a most exciting evening.*"

The highly incriminating cocktail

No mention of any alcohol before that dinner, but since for tea—and pause here to note that if ever a character was late for tea you could be sure they had been up to something pretty suspicious—they had already consumed 'a plate of freshly baked scones of most appetizing appearance' they almost certainly had knocked back that incarnation-of-the-thirties drink, a cocktail. Though fictional people then seemed less dependent on alcohol than characters in today's books. When the Chief Constable in *Death Is No Sportsman* breaks the news to the widow, 'Afraid this is a terrible shock to you,' he says, 'can I get you a glass of water or something?' But if E. R. Punshon passes over the cocktail before dinner, other authors make ample recompense, often with a pointed older-generation jibe about this 'disgusting modern habit' replacing traditional sherry.

At the top of our social scale, which began with prep school masters and only baulked at royalty, the cocktails would be shaken by that oft-recurring figure, the male secretary. And, if he was about, you could do a lot worse than plump for him as the murderer. He had the notable advantage, since he was in a subordinate position, of being neutral in the sympathy stakes while still being a gentleman, necessary qualification for anyone who done it. John Dickson Carr, himself the originator of a plentiful stream of books featuring the Chesterton-like Dr Gideon Fell, found in some 1935 statistical analysis that 'Secretary' was the most common occupation of any murderer.

When the cocktails were not being dispensed by the murderous private secretary they were often being tossed off, with terrible bravado, in night-clubs. Bravado because in all likelihood, in the words of *Hamlet, Revenge*, 'in the midst of frolic, certain stalwart and hitherto most frolicsome gentlemen disentangle themselves from false noses, paper caps, balloons and streamers, bar the available exits and admit a bevy of uniformed colleagues to count the bottles, sniff at the glasses and take down names and addresses.'

Undertones of war

But this is how, tirelessly defying a ridiculed law for all the world like so many pot-smokers of today, the rich lived, unexceptionable clubmen and gentlemen of private fortune. And, of course, officers. For, though these books were written on the eve of the 1939-45 War, traces linger by the score of the perhaps more tragic affair of 1914-18. A war record was a handy way of making the reader believe, as truth or red herring, that a character was a goodie or baddie or of showing the hidden bravery beneath the placid exterior of solicitor or don. Not a little, too, of the Army hierarchy survived in chance comparisons like 'the inevitable sense of constraint the presence of a commanding officer entails'.

Yet World War II, for all that our writers plainly did not intend to thrust unpleasantnesses at us, cast its shadow before. 'Dictator' is a word to be found here, there and everywhere like self-sown forget-me-nots in easy-going gardens. The leader of a gang in Nicholas Blake's prep school is dubbed the 'Dictator'. Anthony Gilbert makes a reference, casual as the phrase 'common as Dalmation dogs in town', to arrangements being made by a private secretary (another!) 'as efficient as a dictator'. And when, in *Death Is No Sportsman*, papers mapping out a business merger enter the plot the parties are said to have been moving 'with all the mutual distrust of two dictators engaged in forming a new "axis".'

Every now and again, too, the catastrophe ahead is cheerfully used to provide a mainspring for the action or, more usually, as a nice red herring. But in principle spies were, as one of the characters in *Hamlet, Revenge* remarks to the detective-story writer, 'a species of excitement your austere art sniffs at'. Sniff we certainly did. Eric Ambler was almost as 'common' in our snob-clouded eyes as the Americans, and despised they were for all that writers such as Ellery Queen were producing, in American settings, books almost

"Cracker Harris straightened himself an' raised his rifle above his head an' yelled: 'Come on an' fight! Come on, you dead men!'"

A war record was a handy aid to characterisation.

precisely similar to the ones we wallowed in. But it was simply not done to read them, which meant that read they were, although nobody ever boasted about it.

The Blitz: and it's 'murder as usual'

When the hinted-at armageddon arrived it did not, as might have been expected, bring to a sudden end the cosy world of what one of its chroniclers, Colin

Watson, has neatly called 'Mayhem Parva'. Indeed, the very opposite happened. Where once Cyril Hare's vicar's wife had said, 'My husband reads a lot of those nonsensical crime novels', now when the bombs began to fall London librarians found, according to W. B. Stevenson, one of their number, that the most used books in the shelter libraries were just these. So writers happily went on providing. Some totally ignored the cataclysm, like Gladys Mitchell's *Laurels Are Poison* which was published in 1942 'in complete conformity with the authorised War Economy Standard'; others took it in their stride, seizing on blackout and firewatching duties as splendid opportunities for alibi-making and alibi-faking.

Take Christianna Brand's still highly enjoyable *Suddenly at His Residence*, published as late as 1947 but set in the latter days of the war. Here an out-of-the-blue flying bomb (though fairly and decently planted) ingeniously solves the awful dilemma of having made the one who done it rather too sympathetic. If you wrote about people with some sympathy (and Miss Brand certainly did), you could not leave out the person your plot had fixed on as the murderer. But having made him (or her) someone your reader felt for, what could you do at the end but something like killing him off through enemy action?

Ingenuity, applied to a literary rather than a criminological problem, generally won through. But, for better or worse, people were now the dominant note. Their presence accounted for that frequently found phrase 'the psychological approach', an adroit device permitting return to the novel's proper task while yet appearing to be producing the puzzles thought to be the source of all popularity. How impossible it would have been in the 1920s to claim, as Nicholas Blake's Nigel Strangeways is made to, 'an intuition which had helped him more than once'. And in 1937 Michael

Innes's Appleby himself declared (showing incidentally that he too was a reader) that detective stories 'always have a psychological drift now'.

The belated arrival of Sigmund Freud

Mr Innes's disciple, Edmund Crispin, (a pseudonym this: was it taken from Scamnum's Crispins, that pleasantly conceived corruption of Crippen?) is equally a swimmer in the psychological drift for all his

fervid tributes to puzzledom and frivolity. 'A crime,' his hero, Gervase Fen, Professor of English Language and Literature in the University of Oxford, murmurs wishfully as *The Case of the Gilded Fly* opens, 'a really splendidly complicated crime.' And the murder that follows is as complex as any addict could wish, with the fatal shot fired from a courtyard in through an open window, out through another and in again through a third. Yet it is with motive that the enormous consequent explanations end, and it is with people, recognizable and attractive, that the book is concerned.

So much so indeed that there is a fearsome disparity between the individuals we meet on the page and the actions some of them commit off it which we get to hear about only in the long chapter called 'The Case Is Closed'. This disparity I once heard called the hermeneutic aspect of the crime novel (once heard never forgotten), hermeneutics being the science of interpreting the hidden meanings of Scripture. But Mr Crispin papered over that gap with an exhilarating pattern of wit, humour, fizz and allusion. With Michael Innes, he is a champion of the quotation game, so much a part of the detective story, though he earned from the Lynx of the London Library the surely over-waspish end-page comment 'Too donnish by half'.

It is with a book from another doughty quotation-ist, Ngaio Marsh, her 1941 *Surfeit of Lampreys*, in many ways the archetype of our new sub-genre, that it is perhaps appropriate to wind up this look at a world gone by. In the end-papers of the Collins Crime Club edition, the publishers, those canny trend-spotters, trumpet another book as 'a story you will not put down even to listen to the news'—ah, those wireless-glued days—but the tribute might well have been used of this hymn of Miss Marsh's set to the tune 'Murder Must Appetize'. And it still had the power to keep me from the sucking arms of the ever-lurking telly.

In the full blast of war the book did not let even the shadow of that calamity cloud its pre-war horizon, a wholly proper acceptance of the limitations. But this does not mean that it did not acknowledge evil. It did so by the very fact that the mystery of who killed the odious Lord Wutherwood, holder of the purse strings for the delightful Lampreys, is in the end solved. Evil was not allowed to triumph. And it is this affirmation that underlay the whole genre's popularity.

Triumphal endings, with the mystery that is proposed neatly solved, give detective stories, too, a shape and a form. This is a literary quality which wayward Englishmen seldom acknowledge, but which nonetheless has a powerful effect. It gives the feeling of satisfied enjoyment as the book is finally closed, and when *Surfeit of Lampreys* ends (and that is only after 316 bubbling pages) with its little New Zealand heroine about to marry the most suitable of the feckless yet genuinely attractive Lampreys, then that feeling booms quietly out in the inner depths.

The hero, Chief Detective-Inspector Roderick Alleyn, is not only possessed of a small private fortune but also notably fulfils the twin requirements of omniscience (he even knows how to deal with the most *enfant terrible* of the Lampreys: you could hardly be more all-wise than that) and omnipotence, displayed in solving a crime of an altogether desirable complexity depending as it does on a split-second decision by the murderer to juggle computer-deftly with the buttons of a lift. Alleyn thus in the recesses of the reader's mind embodies, first, the fallible being who can yet thwart evil, the knight-errant of old; second, the hunter in all of us who, when foxes are hard to come by, needs vicarious exercise; and finally the Spirit of the Rational asserting in a world of doubts and mysteries that the human brain can do mighty things.

It is the Lampreys, unimpeachably upper class, who generically provide the mandatory background, free-and-easy aristocratic behaviour (listening under doors, if not at keyholes, permitted) in silent contrast to the stuffy accepted pattern. Now almost of archaeological interest, it is still a mine of delights. Yet, though presented en masse, all the family are credibly characterised as people.

'The whiff of another time'

People. That brings us full circle. People were the key to these stories because it is the continuing actions of people faced with some situation that seems to call for response that constitute, precisely, a story. And the story is a drug of powerful attraction to almost everybody there has ever been. The presence of people, indeed, was the trickle of salt that made appetizing the great pie of the puzzle book, sometimes in itself of lumpen indigestibility. That salt, too, made the pie something that often would keep long and well. So that in the end we can go back to them, the best of these books of the halcyon age, and find not only lively enjoyment but the whiff of another time, when things did not seem so serious, when it was pleasant and easy to play, when frivolities did not smack of hectic scamperings under a doom-heavy sky but were innocent and fresh and altogether proper. Long, long live then the detective story.

A connoisseur's guide to the
authors of the appetizing murder

MARGERY ALLINGHAM (1904-1966) was meant to be a
writer from the beginning. Describing her Essex
childhood she once said: "My father wrote, my
mother wrote, all the weekend visitors wrote and, as
soon as I could master the appallingly difficult business of making the initial marks, so did I." At the
Misses Dobsons' Academy at Colchester she learnt
only how to enter a drawing room and how to sit
down at a piano, but her infant inkiness was allowed
plenty of play. At Perse High School, Cambridge, she
staged an immense drama of her own composition,
but left at fifteen to write for *Sexton Blake* and *Girls
Cinema*. At sixteen she received through psychic
means ten different versions of a seventeenth-century
pirate's life which she transcribed as a romance *Black-
erchief Dick,* her first book. Next she wrote a thriller
Crime at Black Dudley in which she created Mr
Albert Campion, then little more than a bouncingly
expressed caricature with a considerable passing like-
ness to the Scarlet Pimpernel, but to develop from a
usefully receptive eye to a very formidable gent indeed. Miss Allingham was married long and happily
to her illustrator, P. Youngman Carter.

H.C. BAILEY (1878-1961), *Daily Telegraph* drama critic and leader writer, was the creator of Dr Reggie Fortune, amiable and life-enjoying consultant surgeon (specialism never recorded). In twenty books or more and dozens of unusually meaty short stories he gave us not only Dr Fortune but the engaging, Bible-quoting, disreputable solicitor Joshua Clunk. Bailey wrote novels, vaguely historical sounding, from 1901 to 1911, but in 1920 turned to crime. His last mystery *Shrouded Death* came out in 1950. Hard to find now, his books are worth disinterring.

JOSEPHINE BELL (1897-) invented Detective-Inspector Mitchell, as well as a medical detective, Dr David Wintringham, featured in more than one of her fifty-nine novels. "Far too many" she says with the severity of manner that underlies a personality of great kindliness. In fact Josephine Bell has created as many detectives as need called for. With two doctor great-grandfathers, it is not surprising she ended as a G.P. herself. She saw doctoring as a chance to meet people "to put into the stories I had written, as a private but continuous activity, from the time I had learned how to write." Married to a doctor, she was mid-way through her first crime story *Murder in Hospital* when her husband was killed in a road accident. So two detective stories a year helped support her four children till she could find time for mainstream novels, of which *Tudor Pilgrimage* was a well-praised historical example.

NICHOLAS BLAKE (1904-1972) was for a time billed as a mystery poet who had turned to detection, but before long he revealed himself as Cecil Day Lewis, finding the pretence hard to keep up as indeed he found any pretence in a life guided by the ferocious poetic honesty that marked the Auden-Spender school of the 1930s. A poetic course that moved steadily, if slowly, upwards via a spell as Oxford Professor of Poetry till in 1967 he was made Poet Laureate, was paralleled by a crime course that moved rapidly to an assured place among the very good. A working publisher at Chatto and Windus, he also for a time reviewed crime in the *Sunday Telegraph*. What endeared detection to him, he once told me, was its strictness of form. ''You get it in the sonnet, you get it in the detective story, you get it in the blurb.'' Blurb composition was his favourite publishing chore.

CHRISTIANNA BRAND (1907-   ) aged almost thirty, had never thought of writing until, working as a demonstrator of Aga cookers, she found herself in such dread of her supervisor that she bought an exercise book and there and then began a story so as to murder her, pausing only prudently to transfer the setting to a dress shop. Fifteen publishers rejected *Death in High Heels;* but Bodley Head, looking for a successor to Agatha Christie, seized on it, printed it unaltered and sold it like a bestseller. Her next book saw the birth of chirpy Inspector Cockrill and the next, set in a military hospital such as her surgeon husband, Roland Lewis, was then working in, was *Green for Danger,* made into an immensely popular film. She has also written historical novels as 'China Thomson', many beautifully ingenious short stories and some decidedly powerful ones and, illustrated by her cousin Edward Ardizzone, delightful children's books.

MILES BURTON (1884-1964). Reference works either omit his name or give little more than some of his book titles, and indeed the identity behind this penname was deliberately kept secret even after the author's death. He began producing detective stories in 1930 with *The Hardware Diamonds Mystery* and finished with *Death Paints A Picture* in 1960. There were some sixty in between. Since his death, it has been revealed that he was none other than John Rhode, q, as they say, v.

JOHN DICKSON CARR (1905-1977) simply rocketed off from the more striking and lovable traits of G.K. Chesterton in order to create one of our favourite sleuths, Dr Fell. Of course, our prolific author also split himself into two, frequently choosing to write as Carter Dickson and thus leaving a fine old bibliographical tangle in his wake. But it has been a fair and frothy wake, right from the start, when this son of sometime U.S. Congressman Woods N. Carr started writing locked-room mysteries set in France with one M. Bencolin as detective, through book after book including the book review column he wrote regularly for *Ellery Queen's Mystery Magazine*. An honorary Englishman by virtue of a long period of residence, especially in sitting out the blitz on Bristol, he once held the position of Secretary in the Detection Club.

AGATHA CHRISTIE (1890-1976), preceded since 1971 by 'Dame', is the one name that is synonymously exchangeable for 'detective-story'. The honour was bestowed for services to literature and, although as Mary Westmacott she has produced a handful of romances (not all that good, they tell me), it was crime-writing alone that earned her the title. Encouragingly for all who aspire in the field, her first book, written after her sister belaboured by story after story of "unrelieved gloom, in which most of the characters died" had bet her she could not produce a decent detective tale, *The Mysterious Affair at Styles* was rejected by six publishers before triumphing at the hands of John Lane. Each succeeding book seemed to hit the nail on the head, a good cliche to describe Mrs Christie's splendid gift for saying the obvious in so exactly right a manner that dullness is avoided and immense popularity ensured. In 1926, when she broke the cardinal rule and made a Watson (Ssssh!) the murderer, she compounded the felony by mysteriously disappearing herself for a short time as the result of a nervous breakdown which ended in divorce from her first husband and brought on herself such a Press hoo-hah that ever since she has been solidly suspicious of all interviews. She subsequently married Sir Max Mallowan, the archaeologist. It had been a long life and one of steady output, with one curious by-product in that her Hercule Poirot, a retired policeman of at least forty in 1916 when he took refuge in England, had to be notching the 100 mark at his final appearance, arthritic but spry, in 1972. (Final in time, that is. The last Poirot, written during the 1939-45 War and kept in a solicitor's safe since, is 1975's ultimate contribution to the saga.) Her other great gift to detective fiction, Miss Marple of the clicking knitting needles, began elderly and ingeniously stays so forever.

G.D.H. COLE (1889-1959) was one of those very remarkable people who incidentally took to crime together with his wife MARGARET (1893-1980), a member of the Postgate family with other members of which G.D.H. collaborated at various times and one of whom, Raymond, wrote that minor crime classic *Verdict of Twelve*. Son of a jeweller, G.D.H. had a luminous career at pre-1914 Balliol, "a dark dynamic presence" said a contemporary, and rapidly made a name in the politics and economics of the Left as an advocate of workers' control. His book *The*

World of Labour had a great success in 1913 and was only the start of a stream of publications that went right on till his death, dense works of statistical research mingling with warmly-felt biographies of such people as Cobbett. Between the wars there was a 'Cole Group' at Oxford that attracted young inquirers who included W.H. Auden, Hugh Gaitskell, John Betjeman. In 1931 he was stricken with diabetes, an illness that made him, in his wife's words, "write faster and faster, larger and more complicated books." It was about this time, and up to 1942, that the twenty-nine detective stories and four volumes of short stories which he wrote, all but one with Margaret, poured out.

EDMUND CRISPIN (1921-1978), whose real name was Bruce Montgomery, is another of Oxford's generous gifts to the crime-reading community, his golden days there being spent in the company of Kingsley Amis (inveterate flirter with the crime story), Philip Larkin, John Wain, Alan Ross and Edward du Cann. His crime output has been disappointingly tricklish, only eight novels in thirty years, though there are some fifty short stories and in 1976 we had the last, *The Glimpses of the Moon*. Under the Montgomery name music poured forth more prodigally, with published concert works and background scores for some forty films as well as for radio and TV.

FREEMAN WILLS CROFTS (1879-1952). Recently members of the Detection Club annually pledged themselves to "hold the banners high alofts Of alibis that test the brains And timetables for railway trains," alofts, needless almost to say, forcefully rhyming with "Freeman Wills (God bless him) Crofts", creator of Inspector French, ploddingest of detectives. Crofts was a civil and railway engineer who retired in 1929, having written his first puzzle story while recovering from an illness in 1919. French, and a few other heroes, lasted him well until his final book *Anything to Declare?* (1957). He was at one time parish-church organist at Coleraine in Northern Ireland and late in life he produced a modern-speech version of the Gospels.

ELIZABETH FERRARS (1907-   ) brought to life Toby Dyke in her first crime book (her first novel had been published some nine years earlier). After six Dykes, Miss Ferrars (She was married in the year of her hero's first appearance to Robert Brown, now Professor of Botany at Edinburgh) "got to hate him so much I dropped him." Splash. However, since then she has given us a steady stream of good grainy murder stories, some fifty books in all, and has entered that quite large and much-to-be thanked band of crime authors who were writing in the good old days and are writing still in today's yet better ones. In America, in response to her publisher's worried request, she is E.X. Ferrars.

MARY FITT (1987-1959) was Miss Kathleen Freeman, D. Litt. And that honour was gained not by writing whodunnits but by studies in Classical Greek, in which she was a Lecturer at the University College of South Wales from 1919 till 1946. Between 1936 and 1959 she wrote more than thirty crime books. She specialised in what one critic has called "a reflective kind of character-detection."

R. AUSTIN FREEMAN M.D., M.R.C.S. (1862-1943), creator of Dr John Evelyn Thorndyke M.D., F.R.C.P., was for a short time in 1901 Acting Medical Officer at Holloway

Prison. He wrote accounts of his earlier travels in Africa and in 1902 collaborated with John James Pitcairn as 'Clifford Ashdown' to write *The Adventures of Romney Pringle*. In 1907 came his own *The Red Thumb Mark*, which introduced a hero who was to gain such a following that the book was eventually reissued as (thrilling title) *The Debut of Dr Thorndyke*. On they rolled afterwards, some forty volumes in all, till *The Jacob Street Mystery* (in America *The Unconscious Witness*—and no wonder) in 1942. Freeman took his art seriously, writing in *The Nineteenth Century* for May 1924 a measured defence of "the detective story, to adopt the unprepossessing name by which this class of fiction is now universally known." It pays brusque tribute to the virtues of characterisation and story but then puts all its weight behind the intellectual element, claiming as the ideal audience "a clergyman of studious and scholarly habit".

ANTHONY GILBERT (1905-1973), who was Lucy Malleson, modestly chose a pseudonym so as to avoid cashing in at all on the reputation of her uncle, the actor Miles Malleson, at the start of a strong name-in-lights phase in 1927 when her first book *Tragedy at Frayne* appeared. From then on she entertained us book after book, year after year, more than sixty in all, often starring her outrageous dodgy solicitor Arthur Crook (Life, plodding away behind Art, came eventually to produce a real Arthur Crook as long-time and most respectable editor of the *Times Literary Supplement*). An early member of the Detection Club, she was its first Secretary.

CYRIL HARE (1900-1958) was the pseudonym used by one of that band of legal lights who in their leisure time have siphoned off their knowledge and experience into the whisky of the detective story. Alfred Alexander Gordon Clark was called to the Bar in 1924 and between 1924 and 1945 was a temporary legal assistant to the Director of Public Prosecutions. In 1950 he was made a County Court judge. In all he published only ten books, but they are each worth reading still. Several feature a pleasant self-deprecating barrister named Francis Pettigrew.

MICHAEL INNES (1906-   ) donniest of the dons' school, is J.I.M. Stewart, Reader in English Literature at Oxford since 1969 and author of several literary studies and a number of mainstream novels (which refrain from doing all they might). Since he burst upon the detection world in 1936 with *Death at the President's Lodgings* (pusillanimously re-titled in America *Seven Suspects*) he has given us some fifty crime books, in recent years unmitigated and self-acknowledged jeux d'esprit, though always apt to contain some dazzling jeux indeed. His hero is John Appleby, who has risen from mere Inspectordom to a knighthood and retirement after a stint (unrecorded) as Commissioner of the Metropolitan Police. He even spawned a detecting heir, young Bobby, though not with great literary success.

RONALD KNOX (1888-1957) was a Balliol contemporary of the darkly dynamic Douglas Cole. A man "of frail drooping figure . . . and unobtrusive chin," says one biographer, deep into theology (his father was Bishop of Manchester and his mother the daughter of a Bishop of Lahore), a-fizz with limericks and failing to get the First confidently expected of him because he neglected to read the prescribed books. Already while at Eton he had broken into print with a volume of verse in English, Latin and Greek. From Oxford he went to the Church of England and wrote theology, mostly in the form of literary parody. Before long he moved across to the Church of Rome in which he took Holy Orders in 1919 and was made a Monsignor in 1936. In 1926 he both became chaplain to the Roman Catholic students of Oxford, a post he held till 1939, and caused a happy sensation by broadcasting a parody bulletin describing revolutionary rioting in the streets of London. Apart from his parodies and his Ximenes crosswords, Ronald Knox produced five rather characterless detective stories, an essay exposing Sherlock Holmes's howler in the matter of detecting the direction of a bicycle from the superimposition of tyre marks (*The Priory School*) and a rationale for the sternly humorous rules of the Detection Club forbidding the use of mysterious Chinamen and confining secret passages to a strict minimum of one per book. And in the meanwhile work went steadily forward on what was to be his magnum opus, a new translation of the Bible, a version sadly now superseded for general Catholic use.

E.C.R. LORAC (1894-1958) I have recorded already my slight sense of shock on discovering that this trenchantly logical, pipe smoke-wreathed hero of my boyhood was Miss Edith Caroline Rivett, elegant practitioner of the arts of embroidery and calligraphy with a stitched tunicle and an illuminated book of benefactors to be seen in Westminster Abbey. She even was also—prolific lady—that decidedly lesser light, as it then seemed to me, Carol Carnac. Why did I never guess? And had I once read her *The Dog It Was that Died* before using that title myself?

Dame NGAIO MARSH (1899-   ) was honoured not for her crime novels, though the body of her work deserves it, but for her services to the theatre in her native New Zealand. Yet it was a literary work, a play, that brought her into the theatrical world. She had taken this to a Shakespearian actor-manager; he rejected the work but recruited the writer. Dame Ngaio (you pronounce the Maori name 'Ny-o') has gone on not just to act but to direct and to lecture in drama at the University of Canterbury. Perhaps something in her blood turned her to crime. "My father," she has written, "is a descendant of an ancient English family, the piratical de Mariscos, Lords of Lundy. They were kicked out of Lundy on general grounds of lawlessness and turned up in Kent [the one permitted secret passage?] where they changed their name to Marsh." The hero of most of the books that began appearing in 1934 (thus making her another of the happily long-lived crime authors who to all our pleasures bridge the gap between a now classical past and the hurly-burly of today) is Roderick Alleyn, named after the actor-manager, Shakespeare's contemporary. Alleyn, a figure of delicious romance, has urbanely proceeded up the ranks at Scotland Yard as well as wooing and marrying the sculptress Agatha Troy (Dame Ngaio studied art at university).

GLADYS MITCHELL (1901-   ) is one more with feet sturdily planted in the past and present whose fiftieth book, published in 1976, *Late, Late in the Evening*, is set in the Cowley, Oxfordshire, where she was born long before the advent of Morris motors. She has also written as Stephen Hockaby. She trained as a teacher at Goldsmiths College, London, and for many years taught English and history while the saga of Dame Beatrice Lestrange Bradley unfolded, often reflecting the author's particular interest in ghosts and witchcraft. Goodwill radiates from the books and Miss Mitchell says charmingly of herself that she is "far too lazy to hate anybody."

E.R. PUNSHON (1972-1956), enormously fecund, left little trace of himself in the reference books of the world, save long lists of titles. His first novel *Earth's Great Lord* appeared in 1901, his last, a crime story, *Six Were Present* came out in 1957. The initials E.R. concealed the names Ernest and Robert, and his *Proof Counter Proof* (1931) was one of the books included by the American critic Alexander Woollcott in his list of titles for the White House.

JOHN RHODE (1884-1964) was another author who put many thousands of words into print but let little of himself appear. Shortly after he died indeed a semi-anonymous E.C. wrote in *The Times* obituary columns: "The recent death of Major C.J. Street, O.B.E., M.C., does not seem to have called forth any appropriate reference to his contribution to the world of letters. *Hungary and Democracy* (1923) was regarded as an important contribution to the series The Story of the Nations, published by Fisher Unwin, and the four books he wrote under the pseudonyms I.O. and F.O.C. are a clue to a gallant military career. But for the last forty years his writing was confined to mystery stories under the pseudonym John Rhode. He was an exponent of the classic mystery story, and each of his seventy-seven books was based on a scientific idea, which only appeared to the master mind of Dr. Priestley . . ."

DOROTHY L. SAYERS (1893-1957) was also a highly reticent person. A first biography disclosed that this daughter of the vicarage became, while working at Benson's advertising agency in the 1920s, the mother of an illegitimate child, a fact which would greatly have embarrassed her later in life when, largely as the result of her then controversial bringing to radio of the voice of Jesus Christ in her series play *The Man Born to be King,* she became a poor person's theologian. Indeed, even her marriage in 1926 to Oswold Fleming, an ex-soldier of little or no occupation, was not generally known about. Her first book *Whose Body?,* written to make some money before she got her job at Benson's, was rejected by more than one publisher chiefly on the grounds of "coarseness" (a substantial clue being the uncircumsized state of the mysterious naked body) but after tactful alteration it was accepted and sold well enough to encourage a second. Success mounted with the Wimsey books following one by one, as well as perhaps her most interesting work (full of clues to the mind behind as well as possessing a considerable theme) *The Documents in the Case* and plentiful short stories including those featuring the unlikely but not unengaging Montague Egg, wine salesman. In the end she tired of her hero, like Conan Doyle, and Elizabeth Ferrars, before her. She did not kill Wimsey off: she married him off (*Busman's Honeymoon,* 1937). He appears thereafter only in one or two ugh-making short stories and a series of imaginary letters written to boost morale in the earliest days of the Second World War. An old edition of Dante, snatched up on the way to the cellar as a wartime doodlebug boomed overhead, led to the monumental venture of making a new translation of the *Divine Comedy,* a task she had not quite completed when death, that force she had so often written of, overtook her.

JOSEPHINE TEY (1897-1952) was another writer to have a great success in a field other than crime. As Gordon Daviot she wrote *Richard of Bordeaux,* a play that ran for over a year with the young John Gielgud in the lead, as well as other dramatic works and a biography of Claverhouse. Her real name was Elizabeth Mackintosh and she spent much of her life as a physical training teacher, though she retired early to look after her father in Scotland. There are ten Tey crime books, of which *The Franchise Affair* is a perennial seller in Penguins.

HENRY WADE (1887-1969). Detective stories are put in their place in the *Who Was Who* entry for Major Sir Henry Lancelot Aubrey-Fletcher, Bart., C.V.O. (1957), D.S.O. (1918), M.V.O. (1910), Grenadier Guards (1908-1920), J.P. for Buckinghamshire and Lord Lieutenant for the county from 1954-61, Standard Bearer in 1956 of H.M. Bodyguard of the Hon. Corps of Gentlemen-of-Arms. It lists under publications *A History of the Foot Guards to 1958* and "author of several novels under the pen name of Henry Wade." There are in fact twenty-three such books.

Of the twenty-seven authors here discussed, thirteen are women, fourteen men. Nine were Oxford graduates, two Cambridge and four were at other universities. One, Agatha Christie, attended no school.

Illustrations to this volume have been selected from the following sources:

Page 6 Collins Crime Club Cover: 7 Collins Crime Club backcover: 12 & 13 Strand Magazine: 15 Mansell Collection: 18 Strand Magazine: 19 Strand Magazine: 22 Strand Magazine: 24 Illustrated London News: 26 Strand Magazine: 27 Strand Magazine: 28 Strand Magazine: 30 Strand Magazine: 33 Strand Magazine: 34 Collins Crime Club Cover: 36 Strand Magazine: 38 Strand Magazine: 40 Strand Magazine: 43 Strand Magazine: 44 Collins Crime Club Cover: 46 Strand Magazine:

Front cover design by Magnus Lohkamp is based on an original Collins Crime Club Cover 'Death at Breakfast' by John Rhode.

Acknowledgements

The publishers are indebted to Collins Publishers and especially Mr John A Ford for researching and permitting us to reproduce the original 'Crime Club' covers that appear in this volume.

Thanks are also due to IPC for permitting the editor to draw freely on the illustrations of the now defunct 'Strand Magazine'.

A final note of appreciation is owing to Mr Dennis Arundell for leading our researchers to the photo-call pictures of the first production of 'Busman's Honeymoon', by courtesy of 'The Illustrated London News'.

The author wishes to thank Frank Arthur, writer of five flavourful mysteries all set in the Fiji Islands, for assistance in compiling the biographical facts about our companions in crime.

PICTURE RESEARCHERS:
Olive Synge and Hazel Lohkamp

LEMON TREE PRESS

SOME MORE TITLES IN THE
Time Remembered
SERIES

Keep Mum!
GEORGE BEGLEY

The Blackmailing of the Chancellor
KENNETH BOURNE

Why Fings Went West
FRANK NORMAN

Pride, Prejudice and Proops
MARJORIE PROOPS

BOOKS PUBLISHED BY THE
MYSTERIOUS PRESS

All books are in print and available from
The Mysterious Press.